Sophia
the Snow Swan
Fairy

For Phoebe Graves, with lots of love

Special thanks to Sue Mongredien

ISBN 978-0-545-38422-3

12 11 10 9 8 7 6 5 4 3 2 1   12 13 14 15 16/0

Printed in the U.S.A.   40

This edition first printing, March 2012

Sophia
the Snow Swan
Fairy

by Daisy Meadows

SCHOLASTIC INC.

New York   Toronto   London   Auckland
Sydney   Mexico City   New Delhi   Hong Kong

There are seven special animals,
Who live in Fairyland.
They use their magic powers
To help others where they can.

A dragon, black cat, phoenix,
A seahorse, and snow swan, too,
A unicorn and ice bear —
I know just what to do.

I'll lock them in my castle
And never let them out.
The world will turn more miserable,
Of that, I have no doubt!

Contents

Into the Darkness

Kirsty Tate bit into a warm, sticky marshmallow and smiled. Yum! It had been another fantastic day at the adventure camp where she and her best friend Rachel Walker were staying for a week. The sun was going down and everyone was sitting around a fire, singing songs and toasting marshmallows. "I'm having such a wonderful vacation," Kirsty said happily to Rachel.

"Me, too," Rachel agreed. Then she lowered her voice. "Especially with our new fairy friends!"

Kirsty smiled at her friend's words. She and Rachel shared an amazing secret. They had met lots of fairies and had shared all kinds of exciting adventures with them! This week, they were helping the Magical Animal Fairies find their lost animals because Jack Frost had stolen them. The girls had already helped the fairies find a young dragon, a magic black cat, a phoenix, and a seahorse . . . but there were still three animals left to return to Fairyland.

"Listen up, guys!" came a voice just then. Kirsty and Rachel turned to see Trudi, one of the camp counselors, standing on a tree stump. "There's such a wonderful full moon tonight, we're going to take a night hike. I have something very special to show everyone. Can you get into pairs, please?"

The campers immediately hurried to pair up. Kirsty and Rachel went together, of course, and smiled at each other. They always had their most exciting times when it was just the two of them.

Two other counselors, Jacob and Lizzy, began passing out flashlights.

"Why are we going hiking in the dark, anyway?" a girl named Anna wanted to know.

"Nature looks very different at night," Jacob told her. "All kinds of birds and animals come out that you don't see during the day. And the surprise waiting for you at the end of the trail will definitely make it worth the walk!"

When everyone was ready, the campers set off, flashlight beams bobbing across the grass. First they went through some dark woods. Because they heard strange scufflings all around them, Rachel and Kirsty kept close together.

Twigs snapped beneath their feet, and

Kirsty stumbled on a long, twisted root. It was a relief when they came out from under the trees and into the open, where the moonlight lit the path and covered everything with a silver haze.

"It's so pretty," Rachel marveled as they walked alongside a bubbling stream. The moonlight glittered on the water as it rushed by.

"And look at that swan!" Kirsty

exclaimed. "It's so beautiful with the light reflecting on its white feathers—almost as if it were shimmering."

Rachel stared thoughtfully at the swan. The little bird did seem to be glowing in the darkness. Its gleaming white feathers sent sparkling reflections into the water all around.

"I think it *is* shimmering," Rachel whispered, clutching Kirsty and pulling her away from the path, so the other campers could pass. "Shimmering . . . as if it were magical!"

Kirsty felt her skin tingle with excitement, and she looked closely at the swan. "I think you're right," she said when she and Rachel were alone. "That must be the magical snow swan!"

Sophia
Appears

The girls watched the little white swan as it sailed gracefully along the stream away from them. With its neck curved in an elegant arch, the bird looked so peaceful on the water. Kirsty and Rachel knew that the magical animals all possessed special powers and helped spread the type of magic that every human and fairy could find within themselves—the magic of imagination, luck, humor, friendship, compassion, healing, and courage.

The fairies trained the young animals for a whole year, teaching them how to use and control their powers. Once their training was complete, the magical animals returned to their families. Then they could spread their special gifts throughout Fairyland and the human world!

"The magic snow swan spreads compassion," Rachel remembered. "That's when you're kind to someone who is sad or hurt, I think, and you try to help them feel better."

"That *is* a nice gift," Kirsty said.

"Well, we'll have to catch the swan somehow and use our fairy dust to take her back to Fairyland." She fingered the gold locket that she always wore around her neck. The fairy queen had given it to her, and it was full of magic fairy dust.

"Good idea," Rachel agreed. "She doesn't look as big as an ordinary, full-grown swan, does she? Hopefully we can scoop her up when she comes near the bank."

The girls crept closer to the stream. The swan was very near the grassy bank now. As she dipped her head slightly to peck at some weeds, the moonlight gleamed on her feathers. Kirsty took a deep breath and inched forward, arms outstretched. Her fingers were just about to touch the swan's white feathers when she stepped on a twig, which cracked with a loud snapping sound.

The swan was startled and threw up her wings, splashing the water as she took off into the air. With just a few flaps, she had flown far upstream.

"Oh, no." Rachel groaned, watching the bird disappear. "Now what? Should we go to Fairyland anyway, to tell the fairies we found the swan?"

"I—" Kirsty began, then stopped. "Rachel—look!" she said. "That flower in the grass . . . it's shining so brightly!"

Both girls stepped closer to the flower. It was bright white, and its closed petals glowed with light. Then, as Rachel and Kirsty watched, the flower petals opened . . . and a tiny fairy fluttered up into the air!

"Sophia!" Kirsty cheered, recognizing the Snow Swan Fairy. She and Rachel had met all the Magical Animal Fairies

at the start of their adventure. Sophia
had long brown hair, fastened at one
side with a purple bow. She wore
a pinkish-purple top that was dotted
with sparkles, and a fluffy
skirt. On
her feet
were
pretty
purple ballet flats.

Sophia flew in a swirly loop
before floating down to hover in front of
Kirsty and Rachel. "Hello again, girls,"
she said with a smile. "I came here
because I could sense my snow swan,
Belle, was nearby. Have you seen her
anywhere?"

"Yes," Rachel replied. "She was right
here on the stream. But when we tried

to catch her, she flew away!"

"You're so smart
to have spotted
her," Sophia
said. "Now
we need to
find her again.
Will you help
me?"

"Of course," Kirsty said.
"Let's—" But before she could
finish her sentence, she heard the sound
of footsteps and she immediately stopped
speaking.

Kirsty and Rachel turned to see Trudi
approaching. Sophia had to dart out of
sight into one of Kirsty's pockets before
Trudi noticed her.

"Girls, what are you doing back

here?" Trudi
exclaimed. "You
need to keep up—
we don't want
anyone to get lost
in the dark."

"Sorry," Rachel said,
feeling guilty. She'd been so excited
about seeing Belle the snow swan and
meeting Sophia that she'd forgotten all
about the hike.

"Come on, let's catch up with the
others," Trudi said. "It won't be long
before we see the surprise—you can't
miss out on that!"

The girls followed Trudi along the trail
and rejoined the group. Both felt glum as
the camp counselor walked beside them.
Kirsty could feel Sophia wriggling in

her pocket and was frustrated that they couldn't talk about Belle and make plans to find her! What if the snow swan had flown far away? They'd have lost their chance to catch her!

The other campers were waiting on a wider stretch of path. As Rachel and Kirsty joined them, Rachel noticed that

Anna looked confused. "That's weird," she was saying to herself, staring across the stream.

Rachel's heart sped up. What had Anna seen? Had she caught a glimpse of Belle the snow swan doing something magical? "What's weird?" she asked Anna.

"I thought I saw a small green creature on the other side of the stream," Anna replied, rubbing her eyes and staring again. "Not a frog—bigger than that. And it was running on two legs, just like a little person!"

Rachel and Kirsty exchanged horrified

glances, both thinking the same thing:
it sounded like Anna had just seen
one of Jack Frost's sneaky goblins. The
goblins would have been sent to look for
Belle, so the girls had to find the snow
swan — and fast!

Down the Waterfall

Anna shook her head and smiled. "The moonlight must be playing tricks on my eyes," she said, smiling. "That—or some little green men have landed from Mars!"

Lucy, Anna's partner, giggled. "I don't think that's the surprise Trudi has planned for us!" she said. "Come on, let's go."

Anna and Lucy set off together, and Kirsty turned to Rachel. "I bet it was a goblin," she murmured.

"Sounded like one to me," Sophia whispered from her hiding place. "We need to hurry!"

Kirsty and Rachel knew that Jack Frost had sent his goblins into the human world to try to find the magical animals before the fairies did. Jack Frost didn't want the animals to spread their special gifts around the world. He wanted everyone to be as miserable as he was. That was why he had stolen the magical animals in the first place— and why he wanted them back again!

Rachel and Kirsty scanned the
opposite side of the stream and all
around them as they went along, but
there was no sign of goblins now. Rachel
could feel
goosebumps
rising along
her arms as
she searched.
It was kind of
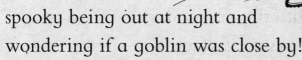
spooky being out at night and
wondering if a goblin was close by!

The stream soon widened and became
a river. After a few minutes of walking,
Kirsty suddenly grabbed Rachel's arm.
"Look," she said. "Straight ahead—it's
Belle!"

Sophia peeked over the edge of Kirsty's
pocket and smiled in relief. "Yes, that's

definitely her," she said in her little fairy voice. "Now, let's think. I need to get her back without being seen."

Rachel bit her lip. "That's not going to be easy," she said in a low voice. "We can't hang back from the others again—Trudi will be upset with us and may even take us back to camp. And, Sophia, I'm worried that if you fly across to meet Belle, someone will spot you glittering in the darkness."

Sophia's pretty face twisted into a frown. "You're right," she said. "Anna already thinks she's seen a strange creature over there. We can't risk her—or anyone else—seeing *me*, too."

The three of them fell deep into thought, watching Belle as she glided serenely down the river. Then Kirsty noticed that the river seemed to come to a stop farther along, with the water dropping over the edge. "It's a waterfall!" she realized, her mouth open in surprise.

The others looked. Kirsty was right!
They could hear the water crashing
down at the bottom of the waterfall,
making a rushing, roaring sound as it
tumbled over the rocks.

"There goes Belle!" Rachel
whispered, trying not to stare too
obviously as the beautiful white bird
opened her wings again and took
flight. She soared over the edge

of the waterfall. "Wow—you can hardly see her through all the spray."

It was true. They had reached the top of the waterfall now, and it threw up such huge clouds of misty spray that it was almost impossible to see the bottom from where they stood. Belle, too, had vanished into the mist.

"Can you all listen to me for a

minute?" Trudi called just then. "We're going to work our way down to the base of the waterfall now. There's a path on your left that we can follow to the bottom. Take your time, because some of the rocks might be wet and slippery."

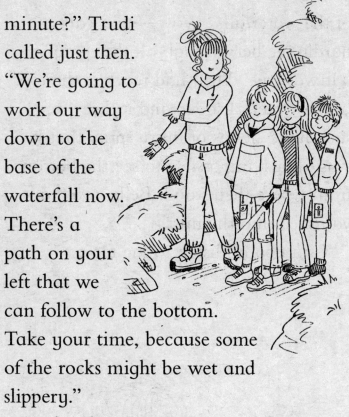

"Is this the surprise?" one of the boys called out curiously.

Trudi smiled. "We're almost to the surprise," she replied. "Just be patient and we'll be there soon! Let's go."

She led the group along a path that
twisted and turned down the side of the
waterfall. Sophia let out a little groan
of frustration. "It's going to take ages to
get down there!" She sighed. "And
Belle could fly miles in that time.
There's only one answer,
girls—I'm going to have to
turn you both into fairies.
That way, we can all
fly together to the
bottom of
the waterfall,
and find
Belle."

She paused, and a flash of doubt crossed her face. "The only thing is, we have to be careful not to fly too close to the waterfall. If our wings get wet from the spray, we won't be able to fly as well . . . which could be very dangerous."

Rachel and Kirsty exchanged a glance. It sounded kind of nerve-racking, diving down to the bottom of the waterfall from such a great height. But then a scuffling noise in the undergrowth nearby reminded them that there were goblins on the prowl. They knew what they had to do!

"OK, let's do it," Kirsty said, looking around carefully to make sure that all the other campers and counselors had already started to make their way down the path. "Let's fly!"

An Icy Trap

Kirsty and Rachel stayed back so
that they were at the tail end of the
group again. Then, when nobody was
looking, Sophia waved her wand over
them, sending streams of fairy sparkles
whirling around. The girls felt a familiar
magic tingle. Moments later, they were
fairies, just like Sophia, with their own
glimmering wings that sparkled in the
moonlight.

"Ready? Then off we go!" Sophia called.

With a deep breath, Kirsty and Rachel plunged toward the heart of the waterfall, keeping a safe distance from the flying spray. They also had to make sure they kept out of sight of the group of campers, who were slowly making their way down the path.

"*Whoaaaaa!*" shouted Rachel. It was amazing, flying down so fast with the world blurring before her eyes. Kirsty was shouting alongside her, although it was hard to hear anything with the noise of the water tumbling below.

It only took a few seconds for the three friends to reach the bottom—and they all gasped as they saw what was there. Stretching through the mist was what looked like a dazzling rainbow!

Kirsty and Rachel knew all about rainbows, of course, from their very first adventures with the Rainbow Fairies. But this was like no other rainbow they'd ever seen. "I don't understand—how can there be a rainbow when it's so dark?" Rachel wondered.

Sophia smiled. "It's a lunar rainbow— or a 'moonbow,'" she explained. "They are very rare in the human world. They only occur when the moon is at its fullest, and when there is moisture in the air."

"Wow," Kirsty said, marvelling at the shining arc of light. "This must be what Trudi wanted to show us. This is the surprise!"

"And there's something even better," Rachel said, pointing excitedly. "I just saw Belle!"

Kirsty and Sophia could also see the magical snow swan gliding away from the waterfall on a new stretch of river. But, unfortunately, they saw something else, too— three goblins on the riverbank.

"Oh, no!" Kirsty exclaimed. "One of them has a wand. What's he going to do?"

The goblin
pointed the
wand at the
river, and the three
fairies watched in dismay as
a stream of icy magic shot out of
it. The frosty stream reached all
the way to the snow swan, like a
jagged bridge of ice.

"Jack Frost must have given them the
wand," Sophia realized. "And he filled
it with his horrible icy magic."

Kirsty and Rachel were alarmed.
They had seen the power of Jack Frost's
magic many times before, especially
when they were helping the Petal
Fairies. The goblins had had a
similar wand then, which had
caused all kinds of problems for

the girls and their fairy friends.

Now the three goblins jumped onto the ice bridge and began skidding clumsily toward Belle.

"Quick, we've got to stop them," Sophia cried, flying ahead as fast as she could. Kirsty and Rachel flapped their wings hard as well, zooming forward at top speed. But they were too late! The goblins slid all the way over to Belle and waved the wand at her. There was a flash of electric-blue sparkles, and then a cage made of icicles appeared around the snow swan. Belle was trapped!

The goblins chuckled with glee and gave each other high-fives. The one closest to Belle picked up the ice cage and tucked it under one arm, and then they all started sliding back to the bank.

Belle's head drooped sadly. The cage was so small she couldn't even open her wings. She began to sing a mournful song that sent shivers down Kirsty's spine. "She sounds so unhappy," she said with concern.

Sophia nodded. "Belle's songs change according to how she's feeling," she said. "When the magical snow swans are very sad, they sing low and deep. When they're happy, they sing at a very high pitch—so high that they can shatter glass." She smiled briefly. "Nobody in Fairyland minds, though, because they are always glad to hear that a snow swan is happy."

"She's not happy now though, poor thing," Rachel said.

Sophia's smile vanished immediately. "No," she said. "She's not. We really have to get her back from the goblins. I want to hear her singing happily again!"

Breaking
Free

Rachel thought hard. "Can your magic melt the bars of the cage, Sophia?" she wondered.

Sophia nodded. "Yes, but we'll need to get very close to the cage for it to work," she said. "Jack Frost's magic is always very powerful. The bars will probably be hard for me to break."

"Maybe we can distract the goblins. Then you'd have a better chance of getting close to the cage," Kirsty suggested.

"Yes, we could buzz around their heads like flies," Rachel added. "They'll be so busy trying to swat at us, you'll be able to sneak over to Belle."

Sophia smiled. "That's a great idea. Let's try it!"

Rachel and Kirsty immediately flew straight for the goblins and began darting in front of their eyes, back and forth, up and down, tickling their big ears with their delicate wings. "Get away from me!" the

goblins grumbled, lashing out at the
fairies. "Buzz off!"

The goblin with the cage was
thrashing around so wildly he almost
slid off the icy bridge. He skidded
forward, slamming into the goblin in
front—and then they both landed on
their bottoms.

Kirsty was so busy annoying the goblins that she almost forgot to watch what Sophia was doing. Their fairy friend was close to the ice cage now, shooting pink sparks from her wand and dissolving the icicle bars one by one. The plan was working!

But no sooner had the thought popped into Kirsty's head, than the goblin with the wand seemed to lose all his patience with Rachel. He zapped her with a stream of icy magic!

Kirsty let out a scream of horror as Rachel froze solid and plunged through the air— heading straight for the cold water of the river!

Luckily, Sophia heard her cry out. The fairy quickly pointed her wand at Rachel and sent a blast of fairy dust in her direction. Just as Rachel was about to hit the water, the fairy dust melted the ice around her, and she was able to flap her wings and soar up to safety. "Thank you!" She gasped breathlessly, her face pale with fright.

"Are you all right?" Kirsty asked, flying over to her. Sophia also left her position at the ice cage and fluttered up to Rachel.

"Quick, let's run!" they heard the

goblins shout. They turned to see the three green figures charging over the icy bridge and back to the riverbank. Then they vanished into the bushes.

"After them!" Kirsty yelled, determined not to let the goblins get away. She, Rachel, and Sophia flew over the river, just as the icy bridge cracked and broke into pieces. Seeing the ice gave Kirsty an idea. "We have to make the ice cage crack open!" she said as they flew. "Sophia, didn't you say that a snow swan's song can be high-pitched enough to shatter glass? Maybe we can get her song to shatter the ice of the cage!"

"Good thinking!" Sophia cried. "And I know a way to make Belle sing in her highest pitch. She and I have a little game we play in Fairyland—I sing the first part of a song and she sings the second. It always makes her so happy that she ends up singing very high!"

"Come on, then, let's catch up with them," Rachel said eagerly. She soared through the air as fast as she could.

It didn't take long before the goblins were in sight. Sophia launched into a melody at the top of her lungs, and they saw Belle lift her head and turn toward

her fairy friend.
The swan
opened her
beak and sang
back to Sophia,
making such
a high sound
that the girls
covered their ears!

Then Sophia sang another melody,
her voice ringing through the air.

Belle responded again, her voice
becoming higher and higher. It was so
high now that the goblin carrying the
cage had to put it down in order to hold
his hands over his ears. On and on Belle
sang, high and true—until the icicles
around her suddenly shattered!

"She did it!" Kirsty cheered, as the swan flapped her wings and took off into the air.

"Oh, no you don't!" the goblin yelled in alarm. He threw himself at Belle, his arms outstretched, and managed to grab her around the middle. "You're not going anywhere," he growled.

A Kind Heart

Rachel felt her shoulders slump with disappointment. Oh, no! Their plan had almost worked perfectly—but she wished that Belle had escaped!

Something very strange was happening, though. Belle had turned her graceful head so that she was looking straight into the goblin's eyes. She began to sing a new song. It was the most beautiful song the girls had ever heard— haunting, melodic, and full of emotion. Beside them, Sophia took in a quick breath. "Belle is singing the song of compassion!" she said. "A snow swan sings this song only if it senses that a person has compassion deep in their heart, compassion that needs to be unlocked."

"You mean . . . she thinks that the *goblin* has compassion inside him?" Kirsty asked in surprise. The goblins were mean and tricky. They usually didn't show kindness toward anyone!

"Let's watch and find out," Sophia

said, her eyes glued to the goblin holding
Belle.

The goblin was listening to the song
as if under a spell. His face softened
suddenly, and his eyes became kind.
"You don't want to be a prisoner, do
you?" he said softly to Belle. Then, in
the next moment, he opened his arms so
that Belle could fly out.

Belle flew straight to Sophia, her neck stretched out. As she flew, her body glittered all over with magic sparkles. She grew smaller and smaller with each beat of her wings, until she was her Fairyland size. She flew into Sophia's arms, and the fairy gave her a delighted hug.

Meanwhile, the other goblins had been watching this in shock. "What were you thinking, letting the swan go?" one of them raged, his hands on his hips.

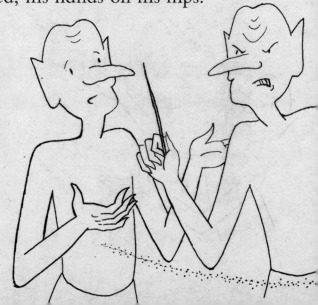

"If I'd known you were going to do that, I'd have used the wand to catch it again!"

The first goblin shrugged. "It felt wrong to keep the swan when she wanted to be with her fairy friend," he replied. "I'm proud of what I did— it was the right thing to do."

The third goblin snorted. "Well, Jack Frost won't think it was the right thing to do!" he argued. "He's going to be really angry!"

The first goblin was smiling at the sight of Sophia stroking Belle's soft feathers. "I don't think I want to work for Jack Frost anymore," he said. "Maybe I'll set up a rescue center to help all the lost and lonely animals of Fairyland." And with that, he walked off, looking very happy.

The second goblin glared at Sophia and lifted his wand, as if he planned to use it. Sophia was too quick for him, though. "If you try any more tricks, I'll get Belle to sing in a really high pitch again," she warned him. "Remember how that hurt your ears last time?"

The goblin looked horrified by the suggestion. "No more singing!" he begged. "My ears still hurt!" Then he and the other goblin turned and ran away into the darkness.

"Just in time," Kirsty said as he vanished from sight. "I can hear the campers coming this way!"

Sophia gave Kirsty and Rachel one last hug. "Thank you," she said. "Now I'd better take Belle back to Fairyland and turn you

two into girls again before I go." She
waved her wand, and magic sparkles
swirled all around Kirsty and Rachel.

Seconds later, they were girls once
again, and found themselves standing
at the back of the group of campers.

When they caught a glimpse of a bright speck of light in the sky just before it disappeared, the girls knew Sophia was on her way to Fairyland.

All around, the other campers were exclaiming about the glittering lunar rainbow that reached across the waterfall.

"It looks almost magical, doesn't it?"
the girls heard Trudi saying. Rachel
and Kirsty grinned at each other. Trudi
had no idea that lots of magical things
had taken place down there just a few
moments earlier!

"I love being friends with the fairies," Rachel whispered to Kirsty as they gazed at the rushing waterfall. She put an arm around her friend's shoulders. "I hope we have another fairy adventure soon!"

Sophia the Snow Swan Fairy
has her magical animal back!
Now Rachel and Kirsty need to help . . .

Leona
the Unicorn Fairy!

Join their next adventure
in this special sneak peek. . . .

spooked!

"Isn't this great, Kirsty?" Rachel Walker turned around in her saddle to smile at her best friend Kirsty Tate. "I've only been horseback riding once or twice before, but now I just love it!" Then Rachel leaned forward and patted her pony, Sparkle.

"Me, too," agreed Kirsty, who was on a beautiful black pony behind Rachel. The girls had been taking riding lessons ever since they arrived at camp, but this was the first time they'd been on a trail ride through the forest. "I think it's because Sparkle and Tansy are so sweet. They don't mind if we do something wrong!"

"Keep following the trail, everyone," Susan, their riding instructor, called from the back of the line. There were several other campers on ponies in front of and behind Kirsty and Rachel. "This path will eventually take us back to the camp."

"I can't believe we only have a day and a half left at camp," Rachel said with a sigh as the ponies ambled

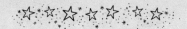

through the forest. It was cool and shady under the trees, but beams of sunlight dappled the grass here and there. "We've had such a good time, haven't we, Kirsty? We've tried hiking, orienteering, and bird-watching, and we've made some great friends."

But Kirsty wasn't really listening. She was staring around, peeking through the trees on either side of the trail.

"Sorry, Rachel," she said quickly. "I was just seeing if I could spot anything unusual. . . ."

Rachel smiled. She knew exactly what Kirsty was looking for! On the day the girls arrived at camp, the king and queen of Fairyland had asked for their help. Kirsty and Rachel had discovered that Jack Frost and his goblins had

kidnapped seven young magical animals from the Magical Animal Fairies. These animals had the power to spread the kind of magical qualities that every human and fairy could possess—the magic of imagination, luck, humor, friendship, compassion, healing, and courage. It was the fairies' job to train the magical animals for a whole year in order to make sure they knew how to use their magic properly. Then the animals would use their incredible powers to bring happiness to both the human and the fairy worlds. . . .

RAINBOW magic™

There's Magic in Every Series!

The Rainbow Fairies

The Weather Fairies

The Jewel Fairies

The Pet Fairies

The Fun Day Fairies

The Petal Fairies

The Dance Fairies

The Music Fairies

The Sports Fairies

The Party Fairies

The Ocean Fairies

The Night Fairies

The Magical Animal Fairies

Read them all!

SCHOLASTIC

www.scholastic.com

www.rainbowmagiconline.com

RMFAIRY5

These activities are magical!
Play dress-up, send friendship notes, and much more!

■SCHOLASTIC
www.scholastic.com
www.rainbowmagiconline.com

HiT entertainment

RMACTIV3